Trees for ALEXANDRE

By Katherine McAleer Bonnel

Illustrated by Nicolas Chirokoff
and Laura Carmona

© Katherine McAleer Bonnel, 2018

© Nicolas Chirokoff and Laura Carmona, 2018 (instagram.com/2tintas_ilustracion)

Text and style editing: Brigitte Neisa and Nancy Boyd McAleer

Acknowledgements: A very special and sincere thanks to Lisa Neisa. Without her vision this project would have never been possible. And to Nicolas Chirokoff for all his patience with the endless changes to the diagramming of the book.

To our beautiful son and guardian angel, Alexandre. Wherever your spirit soars, know your parents will always love you dearly.

And to his sister, Caroline, who helped us see the light in the darkness.

Once upon a time, there was a magical land far, far away where the sun always shone, a gentle breeze always blew, the flowers always blossomed, and the birds always sang. In this land, the trees always welcomed children to play in them, adults to rest in their shade, and animals to find shelter or live there.

In this far away land there lived a king and queen.

While this Kingdom had had other kings and queens before, this king and this queen were very special and loved very much by everyone.

And they had a son, Prince Alexandre, and a daughter, Princess Caroline.

As with everyone in this land, the king, the queen, the prince, and the princess lived a very happy life.

After breakfast, which the four of them always had together, Prince Alexandre and Princess Caroline would usually go and play outside. Not only were the prince and princess brother and sister, they were also the best of friends and did everything together.

Some of their favorite things to do when playing after breakfast -- and also often after lunch, but never after dinner because it would be too dark to play outside -- were picking flowers, climbing trees, playing hide-and-seek and organizing exploration expeditions. After dinner was also when the king and queen would play music, read, plan a trip or do other fun things with Prince Alexandre and Princess Caroline.

One day, as the family was finishing breakfast they heard a loud knock on the door. "How strange," thought the king and queen, "we're not expecting anyone, who could this be?"

The king stood up and opened the door. A gentle looking old man was waiting outside.

"Good morning, I'm sorry to interrupt," said the old man kindly, "but I have an urgent message from the Universe. Prince Alexandre is needed for a very important mission and must come with me."

"There must be some mistake," said the king and queen with looks of shock on their faces, "Prince Alexandre belongs here with us and Princess Caroline. He cannot go with you."

"I know this is difficult to understand," said the old man (who was now inside sitting at the table), "but it must be this way. Do not worry, though, Prince Alexandre will be well taken care of and will discover even more beauty and happiness than here in this Kingdom."

"While you will not be able to see or play with him, he will always be with you in spirit and will never leave your side."

"I can give you until sundown to be together and to say your goodbyes, and then we must go." With that, the old messenger got up and went outside to wait in the shade.

"This cannot be!" exclaimed the king and queen. "What shall we do without Prince Alexandre? He is part of our family and we will miss him too much!"

"I don't want you to go either," whispered Princess Caroline holding her brother's hand, "I will also miss you too much."

"I don't want to go either," said Prince Alexandre, who suddenly seemed wise beyond his years, "but if the Universe says it has to be this way, then I must go. But as the messenger said, I will always be with you; all you have to do is close your eyes and I will be there. I will always be accompanying and protecting you from my special place. Please do not be sad for me, it will make it harder. Be happy that I am in a good place, and will be waiting for you when you come to meet me some day."

The king and queen and their family were so loved, that word spread immediately about Prince Alexandre's special mission for the Universe. Everyone came to hug him goodbye and let the king, queen and Princess Caroline know that if they needed anything, they could count on the entire Kingdom.

Many people also told the king and queen that since Prince Alexandre loved playing in the trees so much they were going to plant trees all over the Kingdom. That way, he would always have a place to rest or play in while on his mission.

The trees would also be a good place for the king, queen and Princess Caroline to sit under and be nearer to Prince Alexandre.

With all the visits from the Kingdom, the day went very, very quickly. Before the king and queen knew it, it was almost sunset. "No!" they thought, "the day has gone too fast, we need more time."

And suddenly, once again, the kind and gentle looking old messenger was at the door. "It's time," he said as he reached out his hand to Prince Alexandre.

The king and queen gave Prince Alexandre one last huge hug to last for a lifetime. Princess Caroline also hugged her brother very tightly. They were very sad, but Prince Alexandre looked them in the eye and whispered, "Remember, if you ever want to feel me or talk to me, all you have to do is close your eyes. I will always be there."

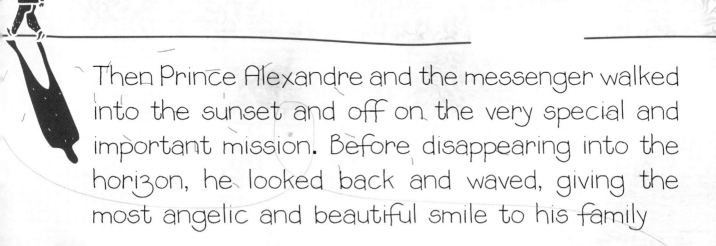

Then Prince Alexandre and the messenger walked into the sunset and off on the very special and important mission. Before disappearing into the horizon, he looked back and waved, giving the most angelic and beautiful smile to his family

The king, queen, Princess Caroline and the entire kingdom felt sad after Prince Alexandre had left because they missed him so very much. It was hard to continue playing and going about daily business because it seemed so strange without the little prince.

As time went on, happiness and laughter began to creep back into the lives of the king and queen and their little princess, but that did not mean they had stopped missing Prince Alexandre. He was always in their thoughts as they had breakfast, played outside, read and played music, or planned a fun adventure somewhere new.

He was certainly in their thoughts when people from all over the Kingdom told them of the beautiful trees that had been planted for Alexandre to play or rest in while on his special mission.

When the king and queen and Princess Caroline could, they would visit the trees that had been planted for the prince. It made them happy he was loved so much that the Kingdom wanted to make sure he always had a place to go.

Sometimes the three of them would come across a beautiful tree that, although not specifically planted for Alexandre, they knew he would love and perhaps stop to play or rest in.

On one very sunny day as the family was having a picnic under their favorite tree in the Kingdom, the breeze suddenly picked up.

The three of them closed their eyes to feel the gentle breeze on their skin and suddenly felt Prince Alexandre's presence more than ever before. While they did not hear his voice out loud, each one could feel him in their heart.

He was reminding them that whenever they wanted to be with him, all they had to do was close their eyes.

After a few moments, the three of them opened their eyes, looked at one another quietly, and then closed their eyes to send all their love back to their beloved prince, son and brother.

Trees for
ALEXANDRE

About the author:

Katherine wrote Trees for Alexandre after her son passed away at birth due to a rare condition developed in utero. The inspiration to write the story came as a way to explain his passing to his twin sister, Caroline, as part of her own healing process and as a way to keep Alexandre's memory alive.

She hopes the book can provide a sense of healing and peace to children and families that have experienced the loss of a twin, child or any sibling.

Katherine and her husband live and work internationally and currently reside in Addis Ababa, Ethiopia with Alexandre's twin sister, Caroline, and younger brother, Maximilien.